Edward
and
THE GREAT DISCOVERY

Courageously written and illustrated by

REBECCA MCRITCHIE and CELESTE HULME

Edward's mother is an archaeologist.
Edward's father is an archaeologist.
Edward's grandmother and grandfather are archaeologists.
And all of them have made very important *discoveries*.

But Edward has *never* discovered anything.
Not a single fossil.
Not a shard of bone.
Not even one piece of treasure.

One night, when rain turned
the ground into mud,
Edward tripped ...

over an *egg*.

What could be inside? thought Edward.

A dinosaur?

A dragon?

Filled with *hope*, Edward rolled
the egg into his house.

He cleaned it.

Kept it warm.

Read to it.

And loved it.

Then one day it *hatched.*

It wasn't a dinosaur. Or a dragon.
It was a *bird*.

A bird that followed
Edward everywhere.
A bird that
helped him.

A bird that *loved* him.

But soon Edward realised that there was something *wrong* with his bird.

It couldn't fly.

His only discovery was *broken*.

So Edward sulked.
And Edward moped.

To cheer himself up,
Edward went to his favourite
place in the world –
The Museum of Ancient Things.

But neither the *giant* whale above him or the *huge* T-Rex skull made him happy.

Labels visible in illustration:
APATOSAURUS is a genus of sauropod dinosaur

WOOLLY MAMMOTH uncovered in Siberia

Then he found himself
in a room he had never
seen before.

A room full of *birds.*

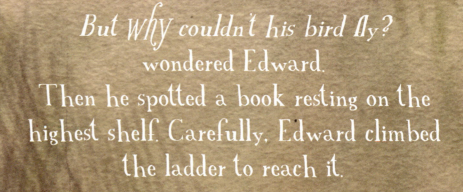

But WHY couldn't his bird fly?
wondered Edward.
Then he spotted a book resting on the
highest shelf. Carefully, Edward climbed
the ladder to reach it.

But just as he touched the book, Edward *fell* ...

safely onto *his* bird's back.

'You're not broken,' said Edward.
'You're a *dodo.*'

'Dodos lived hundreds of years ago. And you're not meant to fly like other birds. You're *special.*'

Edward had made a
great discovery ...

about *friendship*.